D0548502

30130505431323

MEET ALL THESE FRIENDS IN BUZZ BOOKS:

Thomas the Tank Engine
The Animals of Farthing Wood
Fireman Sam
Joshua Jones
Rupert
Babar
James Bond Junior

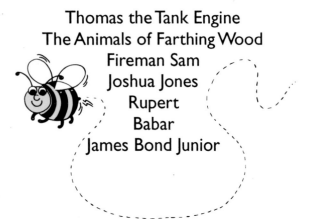

First published in Great Britain 1993 by Buzz Books,
an imprint of Reed Children's Books
Michelin House, 81 Fulham Road, London SW3 6RB
and Auckland, Melbourne, Singapore and Toronto
Reprinted 1993 (Three Times)

The Animals of Farthing Wood © 1979 Colin Dann
Storylines © 1992 EBU
Text © 1993 William Heinemann Ltd
Illustrations © 1993 William Heinemann Ltd
Based on the novels by Colin Dann and the animation series
produced by Telemagination and La Fabrique for the BBC
and the European Broadcasting Union.
All rights reserved.

ISBN 1 85591 2813

Printed in Italy by Olivotto

A New Friend

Story by Colin Dann
Text by Mary Risk
Illustrations by The County Studio

Fox and Vixen were catching rats.

"This is good," said Fox. "It's been weeks since I hunted. I wish I could stay here with you, but I must go and find my friends again."

He told Vixen about the animals of Farthing Wood, their long journey to the nature reserve, and how he had lost them.

"Don't you eat the mice and rabbits?" asked Vixen, amazed.

"They're my friends," said Fox. "We travel together.I couldn't hunt them."

Vixen shivered. "People hunt foxes around here, with horses, and hounds, and whips, too."

"We'll have to be careful," said Fox.

Not far away, a group of very tired animals
were following a huffing, puffing Toad
up a steep hill.

"Nearly there, mateys!" croaked Toad.

"Let me get down, Badger," said Mole.
"You're so tired. I can walk the last bit."

"Nonsense, Moley," rumbled Badger.
"You're no trouble. Half the time, I don't
even know you're there."

But he was talking to himself. Mole had
already slipped off his back, and was
struggling feebly up the hill.

Adder slithered past him. "Lossst your
transsssport?" she hissed.

Weasel jumped over him. "Ha! Ha!
Moley's lost!" she jeered.

"Oh dear! Badger, help!" called Mole.

9

Fox had picked up the scent of his friends.

"They're near here!" he called to Vixen.
He ran back to her. "Will you come with
me?" he asked. "I'd like you to be my mate,
then we could always be together."

Vixen hesitated. "Perhaps," she said. "I'll
decide as we go along."

"Let's go then," said Fox as he followed
the scent. He was full of hope.

10

But further on, the scent divided.

"They must have doubled back," said Fox. "I hope they haven't got lost."

"You follow one trail, and I'll follow the other," Vixen suggested, and she raced off.

"You will come back, won't you?" Fox called after her.

Vixen didn't reply.

The trail took her into the wood, where she noticed a thrush feeding her babies.

"Don't you miss your freedom?" asked Vixen thoughtfully.

"I haven't time," said Thrush, stuffing another worm into a hungry little beak.

"I don't know what to do," sighed Vixen.

"Met a male fox, have you?" said Thrush. "Is he brave? And true?"

"Probably," said Vixen.

They both laughed.

"If you don't try, you'll never know," Thrush told her.

"Thank you, Thrush," said Vixen.

Suddenly, the sound of a horn echoed through the wood.

"The hunt!" Vixen whispered, her body trembling in terror.

"Run! Run for your life!" shrilled Thrush.

Poor Mole was still battling up the hill.

"Help! Badger!" he bleated feebly.

The ground shook beneath him, and a frightful thundering noise made him jump.

"Oh dear! An earthquake!" yelped Mole.

Kestrel saw him, and hovered overhead.

"Keep going, Mole! You're nearly there," she called.

Mole reached the top at last.

"Moley, there you are!" said Badger.
"I was worried. Why did you get off me?"

"Oh, Badger," sobbed Mole. "You were so
tired, and I wanted to help, and oh dear,
I've been a nuisance again."

"Kee! Kee! The hunters have picked up a
scent," said Kestrel.

The hounds bounded into the wood. Their noses twitched at the scent of the foxes. They panted with excitement.

Then they stopped, confused. There were two trails. There must be two foxes!

The Master galloped up. "That way!" he ordered, pointing with his whip.

The hounds set off on Vixen's trail.

Vixen ran faster than she had ever run before. Her breath came in heaving gasps and her legs felt heavy. She was exhausted.

"There's no way out! They'll get me!" she thought desperately.

Fox had run from the hunt, too. He started
to race up the hill, but when he looked
back he could see Vixen breaking out of the
trees. The hounds were closing in!

"I must save her! I must save Vixen!"
he thought, and he ran back down the
hill straight towards the hounds.

The animals on the hilltop saw him go.

"It's Fox! Our Fox!" gasped Badger.

"What's happening?" piped up Mole.

"Kee! Kee! He's trying to head off the hounds to save the vixen!" said Kestrel. "But some of the hounds are still after her!"

"Oh, my poor nerves," squealed Father Rabbit, and he fainted.

Fox raced back up the hill. He was tiring.

"If I can only - reach - the wood at the top of the hill!" he panted.

He could hear the hounds behind him. They were gaining quickly!

"I'm done for," thought Fox. "Oh Vixen, Vixen, I hope you're safe!"

The animals watched in terror.

"He's leading the hunt to us!" howled
Weasel, and she jumped into a bush.

"He hasn't seen us yet," said Badger.
"Stand firm, all of you. Get ready to fight!"

"But we'll be torn to pieces," shrieked
Weasel, from inside her bush.

"Owl! Kestrel! Do your best," said Badger.

21

The birds flew out of the wood, swooping
and diving on the Master and his hounds.

"I say, get the hounds back," called the
Master. "Let's go for the other fox."

The hunt retreated down the hill, and Fox
crawled, exhausted, into the wood.

"Fox! It really is you!" said his friends, crowding round him.

"Kee! Kee! Don't worry, you're safe," said Kestrel. "They've gone after the vixen."

"I've failed her, then," groaned Fox.

"What do you mean?" said Badger gently.

"I wanted her to be my mate," wept Fox.

"Bet she gets away," cackled Weasel. "Three to one odds. Any takers?"

"Weasel," growled Badger. "Shut up!"

Vixen was out of the wood now, and using the last of her strength to run up the hill. Her flanks heaved and her tail drooped.

Then she fell. In a flash, the Master's horse was on her. He lifted his whip, ready to strike Vixen's head.

Fox could do nothing to save her. "I can't look," he said, hiding his face.

Then something small and slim and
slithery slipped through the grass. It was
Adder. She reared up, and sank her fangs
into the horse's foreleg.

The horse shied, whinnying in pain.

The Master lost his seat and fell heavily.
He lay still on the ground. The hounds
milled around in confusion. The other
huntsmen ran up.

"Call off the hunt," one said. "The
Master's hurt."

The horn sounded again. The hunt turned
away, the Master limping along behind it.

Silently, Vixen slipped into the wood.

"What's going on?" asked Father Rabbit, waking up from his faint.

"Fox and the vixen are safe," said Badger with a sigh of relief. "The hunt is over."

"Why did they go?" asked Weasel.

"Kee! Kee!" said Kestrel. "I saw a snake strike at the horse's leg."

"Ha ha! Adder's a heroine!" sniggered
Weasel. "Who'd have thought it? Ah ha ha!"

"It wasss sssome other ssstupid sssnake,"
said Adder, looking embarrassed.

"Don't believe you! Can't fool me!"
chanted Weasel.

"Fox," said Vixen shyly. "You saved me!"

Fox nuzzled her. "Vixen, will you...?"

"Yes," said Vixen. "I'll be your mate."

Badger stepped forward. "Welcome, my dear," he said. "You're one of us, now."

Fox nuzzled Vixen again. "Now we can go to the nature reserve together, where we'll always be safe."